ENCYCLOPEDIA BROWN
THE CASE OF THE DEAD EAGLES
and Other Mysteries

Other APPLE® PAPERBACKS
you will want to read:

About the Author
Donald J. Sobol has been a writer for twenty-five years. In that time, he has written fifty books, including fourteen Encyclopedia Brown titles. He is also the author of a new mystery series about Angie Zane. The first book, *Angie's First Case*, is available in an Apple Paperback edition from Scholastic Inc. Born and raised in New York City, Mr. Sobol now lives in Miami, Florida with his family.

ENCYCLOPEDIA BROWN
BROWN
THE CASE OF THE DEAD EAGLES
and Other Mysteries

by
Donald J. Sobol

Illustrated by
Leonard Shortall

AN
APPLE ®
PAPERBACK

SCHOLASTIC INC.
New York Toronto London Auckland Sydney Tokyo

ISBN 0-590-32565-5

Text copyright © 1975 by Donald J. Sobol. Illustrations copyright © 1975 by Thomas Nelson Inc. All rights reserved. This edition published by Scholastic Inc., 730 Broadway, New York, NY 10003, by arrangement with E.P. Dutton Inc.

12 11 10 9 8 7 6 5 4 3 2   3 4 5 6 7/8

For Jeannine and Fred Zacharias

Contents

The Case of the Dead Eagles

In all the world there was no place like Idaville, U.S.A.

Idaville looked like many other seaside towns. It had beautiful beaches, three movie theaters, and four banks. It had churches, synagogues, and two delicatessens.

What made Idaville different was a red brick house at 13 Rover Avenue. For there lived Encyclopedia Brown, America's Sherlock Holmes in sneakers.

Because of Encyclopedia, no one in Idaville

—child or grown-up—got away with breaking the law.

Encyclopedia's father was chief of the Idaville police. People all over the world, including China, thought he was the smartest police chief in history.

Chief Brown knew better.

Whenever he came up against a case that no one on the force could crack, he put on his cap and went home to dinner. Before the meal was over, Encyclopedia had solved the case.

Chief Brown would have liked to shout from atop the stone heads carved into Mount Rushmore: "My son belongs here!" But what good would it do?

Who would believe him? Who would believe that the mastermind behind Idaville's war on crime was ten years old?

So Chief Brown kept secret the help he got from his only child.

Encyclopedia never said a word, either. He didn't want to seem different from other fifth graders.

But there was nothing he could do about his nickname. He was stuck with it.

Only his parents and his teachers called him by his real name, Leroy. Everyone else in Idaville called him Encyclopedia.

An encyclopedia is a book or set of books filled with all kinds of facts from A to Z—like Encyclopedia's head. The boy detective had read more books than anyone in Idaville. When he breathed fast, his pals swore they could hear pages turning.

Encyclopedia's quick mind was in demand wherever he went. Not only did he solve cases at the dinner table, but often he was called upon to clear up a mystery when he least expected.

Take, for example, the night he and Charlie Stewart were camping overnight in the state park. They had just pitched their tent when they heard a gunshot.

"Gosh," exclaimed Charlie. "That wasn't far away!"

Encyclopedia threw a log on the fire. He pretended that he hadn't heard a thing.

"It can't be a hunter," reasoned Charlie. "Hunters aren't allowed near the campgrounds."

Encyclopedia slid a marshmallow onto a stick and turned it above the fire. Charlie stared at him in surprise and disappointment.

"Don't you think we ought to *do* something?" Charlie said. "I mean, somebody might have been murdered. "

At times like this, Encyclopedia wished he had never become a private detective.

"Catching a murderer isn't like recovering a stolen bike," he said. "A murderer can stop a person's growth in a terrible hurry."

"But somebody might be hurt and need your help," insisted Charlie.

Encyclopedia sighed. "All right, let's go."

The boys walked through the woods, following a path that led in the direction of the gunshot. After a quarter mile, they reached a clearing. At the far end was a cliff about forty feet high and seventy feet wide.

Encyclopedia suddenly stepped to the edge

Encyclopedia dropped to his knees beside a golden eagle.
It was dead.

of the path. He dropped to his knees beside a golden eagle. It was dead.

"This explains the gunshot," he said, feeling anger and sorrow over the senseless killing.

He looked about the clearing. The setting sun seemed to be resting atop the cliff. He had to shade his eyes before he saw the nest. It was in a cottonwood snag halfway up the cliff.

He pointed out the nest to Charlie. Then he said, "I'll bet Mike Bailey is in the park."

"What has Mike to do with the eagle?" said Charlie.

"Don't you remember last year?" asked Encyclopedia.

A year ago, two golden eagles had built a nest in a cottonwood snag lower down on the same cliff. Soon afterward, both birds were shot during the night.

"About nine o'clock, an hour before the shooting, a scoutmaster noticed Mike Bailey standing on this path," said Encyclopedia. "Mike carried a rifle."

"The scoutmaster could have been mistaken," said Charlie. "It was dark."

"No, there was enough light," replied Encyclopedia. "The moon was full."

Charlie scratched his head. "I wonder about that new nest," he said softly. He walked to the cliff and inched his way up. After a hard struggle, he got his chin above the nest.

"There are two eggs inside," he called down.

The news made finding the mysterious hunter more important than ever. The eagle lying near the path was male. The shot that killed him probably had frightened off his mate. Once she recovered, she would return to hatch the eggs.

"We've got to find the hunter before he shoots the mother eagle, too," said Encyclopedia.

The boys had only one lead—Mike Bailey. He was sixteen and rode a motorcycle. It was dark when they found him at campsite 32.

He had pitched his tent and was reading a

hot-rod magazine by the light of the kerosine lamp. Encyclopedia made out a green motorcycle behind the tent. A rifle lay against the black leather seat.

"Going hunting tonight?" inquired Encyclopedia.

"Naw, I just keep the gun handy," said Mike. "I might see a rattlesnake."

"I don't like guns," said Charlie. "Hunting is cruel unless you need food. And killing wildlife for fun is like murder."

"Oh," said Mike. "You're one of those mouthy kids who believes guns should be outlawed."

"I believe we should have better laws to control guns," said Charlie.

"A gun doesn't shoot by itself," replied Mike sharply. "A gun does what its owner makes it do. Don't control guns, kid. Cure the bad owners."

"You can say the same nonsense about automobiles," said Encyclopedia.

Mike stiffened. "Nonsense? Just what do you mean?"

"An automobile does what its owner makes it do," said Encyclopedia. "So while you're curing bad owners, get rid of all automobile laws—speed limits, traffic signals, drivers' tests, fines, and jail terms."

"Move on, wise guy," growled Mike.

Encyclopedia stood his ground. "A golden eagle was shot in the clearing by the cliff less than an hour ago," he said. "If you shot it, your rifle will still smell of powder."

"Take one step nearer my rifle and I'll break your leg," warned Mike.

"Last year two eagles were shot in the same clearing," said Charlie. "A scoutmaster saw you studying their nest earlier that night."

"So I heard," said Mike. "I was out walking—and I had my gun along in case I saw rattlesnakes. I stopped to admire the full moon, which was right above the cliff. I didn't notice the nest, and I didn't shoot any eagles!"

"You can't help where the moon is," said Encyclopedia. "But you can help lying!"

WHAT WAS MIKE'S LIE?

(*Turn to page 87 for the solution to* The Case of the Dead Eagles.)

The Case of the Hypnotism Lesson

Throughout the year, Encyclopedia helped his father solve crimes at the dinner table. When school let out for the summer, he decided to help the children of the neighborhood as well.

So he opened his own detective agency in the garage.

Every morning after breakfast he hung out his sign.

Business was slow on Thursday until Dave Foster walked in. Dave was seven and full of questions.

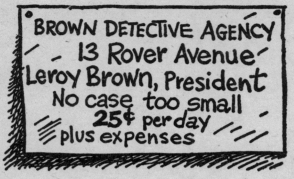

"How do you tell a boy lobster from a girl lobster?" he asked.

"The girl lobster has a longer tail," replied the boy detective.

The answer wasn't worth twenty-five cents. Encyclopedia waited for more questions.

Instead, Dave said, "I think Bugs Meany cheated me."

"If I know Bugs, he did," said Encyclopedia confidently.

Bugs Meany was the leader of a neighborhood gang of tough older boys. They called themselves the Tigers. They should have called themselves the Mountaineers. They were never on the level.

"If Bugs had his honesty taken out, it would be a one-minute operation," said Encyclopedia. "What did he do now?"

"He charged me a dollar to learn how to hypnotize a lobster," said Dave.

"Go over that again," said Encyclopedia.

Dave explained. An hour earlier, he had passed the Tigers' clubhouse. Bugs and his pals had just returned from catching lobsters. They were seated around a boiling kettle, feasting.

"Bugs told me that he had caught eleven lobsters by hypnotizing them," said Dave. "He asked if I wanted to learn the secret for a dollar."

"It was an offer you couldn't refuse," said Encyclopedia.

"I thought so," said Dave. "Bugs picked up a big lobster, the kind you pay a lot of money for in a restaurant. He waved his left hand at it."

"The waving was for show," said Encyclopedia. "He probably was squeezing the nerve centers on its back with his right hand."

"No," said Dave. "He held it up by the tail and muttered a lot of hocus-pocus. It didn't move a muscle. Finally, Bugs said, 'Okay, lobster, are you going to do your stuff or do you want to go into the hot pot?'"

"With a choice like that, what's a lobster going to do?" said Encyclopedia.

"I wouldn't know," said Dave. "All Bugs did was talk. He said a hypnotized lobster could stand on its head while balancing a Ping-Pong ball on its tail."

"And pass out business cards at the same time," added Encyclopedia. "Oh, that Bugs!"

"I didn't get to see one trick," complained Dave. "Bugs said that my dollar paid only for a sample lesson. He told me I could start the course next week—for ten dollars."

Dave laid twenty-five cents on the gasoline can beside Encyclopedia.

"I want to hire you to get back my dollar," he said. "Bugs didn't teach me enough to hypnotize an eggplant. All I got for my money is this."

Bugs held up a large red lobster by the tail with his left hand.

He handed Encyclopedia a color photograph. It showed Bugs and Dave standing together. Bugs held up a large red lobster by the tail with his left hand. He aimed the fingers of his right hand at it like a magician.

"Rocky Graham, one of the Tigers, snapped the picture with a self-developing camera," said Dave. "Rocky told me to show it to my friends and tell them about the lessons."

"What a gyp!" said Encyclopedia. "Let's pay Bugs a visit."

The Tigers' clubhouse was an unused tool shed behind Mr. Sweeny's Auto Body Shop. Bugs and two of his Tigers were still eating lobsters when Encyclopedia and Dave arrived.

"Make like a drum and beat it," snarled Bugs.

"Give me back my dollar first," blurted Dave. "When you took it, you didn't tell me I'd need more than one lesson to hypnotize a lobster."

"Man, oh, man!" exclaimed Bugs. "Nobody can learn overnight. It took me weeks."

"You didn't make that dumb old lobster do one trick," said Dave.

"That's because it was a girl lobster," replied Bugs. "I told you, girl lobsters are hard for boys to hypnotize."

Dave suddenly looked glum. "Yeah, I forgot..."

"I'd like to see you make it do a trick for me," put in Encyclopedia.

"Sorry," said Bugs. "I ate it. In fact, me and the boys are eating the last of the catch right now."

"You big goon!" cried Dave. "You ate the evidence on purpose!"

"Never mind, Dave," said Encyclopedia. "We have enough proof that Bugs cheated you."

WHAT WAS THE PROOF?

(Turn to page 88 for the solution to The Case of the Hypnotism Lesson.)

The Case of the Parking Meters

Bugs Meany had one goal in life. It was to get even with Encyclopedia.

Bugs hated being outsmarted. He longed to pound the top of Encyclopedia's head till the detective could pull up his socks by lifting his eyebrows.

But Bugs never used force. Whenever he felt like it, he thought twice about Encyclopedia's partner, Sally Kimball. Once for each of her fists.

Sally was not only the prettiest girl in the fifth grade, but the best athlete. She could do what Bugs never dreamed possible. Flatten him.

Whenever they fought, the toughest Tiger ended on the ground mumbling about railroad crossings.

"Bugs won't forgive you," Encyclopedia warned Sally. "He'll never live down the lickings you gave him."

The two detectives were seated in the Brown garage. They were discussing the mysterious telephone call each had received during the week.

Monday a boy had called and asked Encyclopedia to meet him on important business at the Indian Burial Grounds at three o'clock that afternoon. The boy did not show up.

Yesterday Sally had received a call from a boy asking her to meet him at the old deserted airstrip at seven o'clock that evening. Like Encyclopedia, she had waited without seeing a soul.

"Bugs Meany is behind this," said Sally. "It's some kind of plot to get revenge."

"There they are!" hollered Bugs. "Mr. Brains and Miss Muscles."

Just then a police car stopped in the driveway. Bugs and Officer Culp got out.

"There they are!" hollered Bugs. "Mr. Brains and Miss Muscles. Private detectives, my eyeball! They should be in jail!"

"What's he shouting about?" asked Encyclopedia.

"Bugs claims that you go along the streets saving drivers from five-dollar parking fines," said Officer Culp. "He says you put dimes in meters and leave a card like this."

He gave Encyclopedia a card. It read:

"Hi! You have just been saved from a $5 parking ticket by the Robin Hood parking aid. Your time on the meter had run out. Could you please send $2 so I may continue to bring you and others this service?"

The card was signed "Robin Hood." The address given was Encyclopedia's home, 13 Rover Avenue, Idaville.

"He must be raking in money," said Bugs. "I'll bet he doesn't report a cent of it to the government!"

Officer Culp seemed uncomfortable. "I'm not sure if any law has been broken," he said. "We'll have to let a judge decide."

"Man, oh, man!" exclaimed Bugs. "The son of our police chief dragged into court! What a disgrace!"

"You don't have a shred of proof," Encyclopedia protested.

"I *had* proof," retorted Bugs. "Monday afternoon about three o'clock I took movies of you feeding a parking meter. But this screwy dame stole the film."

"I did what?" gasped Sally.

Officer Culp broke in. "Bugs claims he picked up the developed film yesterday. At seven o'clock in the evening he showed it in his living room to his pals."

"Just as the film ended, you jumped through the window," Bugs said to Sally. "You grabbed the reel right off the movie projector."

"You're lying through the hole in your head!" cried Sally. "This is a dirty trick to get us in trouble."

"I chased you across my backyard," went on Bugs. "When you passed under the streetlight, I saw that you didn't have the film anymore. You must have got scared and tossed it away in the dark."

"Where were you Monday at three o'clock?" Officer Culp asked Encyclopedia. "And where were you yesterday at seven?" he said to Sally.

Encyclopedia explained about the telephone calls that had drawn him to the Indian Burial Grounds and Sally to the old airstrip. Neither of them had a witness.

"Some alibis!" jeered Bugs. "I've heard better ones from a horse with lockjaw."

Officer Culp decided to settle the argument by driving the children to Bugs's house. He had them search the backyard for the missing reel of film.

After two minutes, Bugs shouted, "I've got it!" He held up a reel of film. "No wonder I couldn't find it before. The wind blew a newspaper over it."

Bugs set up a movie projector and screen in

his living room. Grinning, he put on the reel, threaded the film, and clicked the starting switch.

Most of the film showed Bugs and his Tigers making muscles at the beach.

The last bit of film was of a boy dressed in sneakers, jeans, and a red shirt like one of Encyclopedia's. He put a coin in a parking meter. Then he tucked a card under the windshield wiper of the car by the meter.

"You saw him with your own eyes!" sang Bugs.

"That doesn't prove anything," objected Sally. "We never saw the boy's face."

She was plainly worried, however.

"That boy looks like you from the back," she whispered to Encyclopedia. "Bugs has really built a case against us."

"No, against himself," said Encyclopedia.

WHAT WAS BUGS'S MISTAKE?

(Turn to page 89 for the solution to The Case of the Parking Meters.)

The Case of the Hidden Will

Tuesday evening Chief Brown sat at the dinner table and stirred his soup thoughtfully. Encyclopedia knew what that meant.

His father had brought home a case he couldn't solve.

"Do you remember Brandon King?" asked Chief Brown.

"He owned the largest lumberyard in this part of the state," replied Encyclopedia. "He died last week in Glenn City."

"What is the mystery, dear?" asked Mrs. Brown.

"Mr. King hid his will," said Chief Brown. "It tells who will get all his money and possessions."

"Doesn't his lawyer know where the will is?" inquired Encyclopedia.

"Yes, but Mr. King swore him to secrecy," replied Chief Brown. "Last summer Mr. King wrote the lawyer ordering him not to tell where it is until ninety days after his death. If the will is not found by then, everything he owned is to go to the magicians' union."

"I visited his home four years ago," said Mrs. Brown. "The basement was filled with all kinds of strange equipment. He had a box in which people disappeared. In another box he could saw a person in half."

"Magic was only one of his hobbies," said Chief Brown. "He was also a champion card player. The walls of his playroom were hung with framed enlargements of every card in the deck."

Chief Brown took a spoonful of soup. Then he went on.

"The chances are that Mr. King's sons will inherit everything. His wife died eight years ago, and he has no other relatives."

"The sons helped him in the business, didn't they?" said Mrs. Brown.

"Yes," answered Chief Brown. "But Mr. King didn't think much of them, I'm sorry to say. In fact, his friends believed that one of the sons was stealing from the business."

"Didn't Mr. King know about it?" asked Mrs. Brown.

"Of course he did, but he never would say which son was the thief," replied Chief Brown. "Whoever he is, he's been left out of the will."

"How can you be so sure?" declared Mrs. Brown. "No one knows where the will is hidden except the lawyer. Did he tell you?"

"No, but he gave me this," said Chief Brown, unbuttoning his breast pocket. He drew out a sheet of paper and handed it to Mrs. Brown.

"Nine months ago Mr. King sent a copy to each of his four sons," continued Chief Brown. "The lawyer received this, the original."

Mrs. Brown peered at the paper. "I'm not certain I understand it," she said, and passed it to Encyclopedia.

On the paper was typed a poem. Encyclopedia read:

> "Four Kings worked for me, if badly.
> One stole when I wasn't about.
> Still, I've willed all I have to three,
> And left the odd king out."

Encyclopedia studied the poem as his mother cleared the soup dishes. She looked at him anxiously while she served the meatloaf and vegetables.

She always expected him to solve his father's toughest cases before dessert. So Encyclopedia ate slowly. He needed time with this one.

"How did you come into the case, Dad?" he asked.

"The four sons visited me this afternoon," said Chief Brown. "They wanted help in finding the hidden will."

"*The four sons visited me this afternoon,*" *said Chief Brown.*

"One of them—the thief—was faking," said Encyclopedia.

"What makes you think that?" asked Mrs. Brown.

"The crooked son really doesn't want the will found, since he has nothing to gain. The poem tells him that he is left out of it. Besides, if the will is found, everyone will learn he is the thief."

"I hadn't thought of that," admitted Chief Brown.

Encyclopedia put down his fork and settled back in his chair. He closed his eyes. He always closed his eyes when he did his heaviest thinking.

Mrs. Brown said, "I don't understand Mr. King. He must have been a nice man to give magic shows at schools. Why should he want to leave his money to the magicians' union rather than to his own sons?"

"None of the sons, even the honest ones, worked very hard," said Chief Brown. "Mr.

King was a demanding father. He was probably disappointed in them."

Encyclopedia opened his eyes. That was the sign that he was ready to ask the one question that would break the case.

"Is there anything odd about one of the sons?" he asked. "I mean, is one different in any way from the other three?"

Chief Brown thought a moment. Then he said,

"Three of them are over six feet tall, but Arthur is much shorter," he said. "Frank is the only one without a moustache. Only John wears glasses. Charles is blond and the others are dark-haired."

"Does that tell you where Mr. King hid his will?" asked Mrs. Brown, puzzled.

"Yes, Dad just added another clue to the ones I already have," answered Encyclopedia. "Mr. King wanted to give his sons a chance at finding the will, but he didn't want to make it too easy for them."

The boy detective forked the last piece of meatloaf from his plate.

"Mr. King," he said, "hid the will—"

WHERE?

(Turn to page 90 for the solution to The Case of the Hidden Will.)

The Case of the Mysterious Thief

Encyclopedia had a chance to solve a mystery at lunchtime when Sally suggested they bike to Mario's Restaurant.

"We've got enough money saved up," she said. "We can pick up a pizza and something to drink and eat lunch by the duck pond."

"A neat idea," said Encyclopedia. "If we have any leftovers, we can feed the ducks."

Mario's Restaurant was on Fourth Street. When Encyclopedia arrived, only four tables were being used. It was ten minutes past noon.

The detectives went to the take-out counter. While waiting to give their order, Encyclopedia had a chance to study the room.

Against the wall stood a row of tables for two, empty except for a middle-aged couple. The man was slender and sat with his back to the wall. Facing him was a beefy woman in a tight brown dress. They were eating spaghetti.

Three men and a very fat woman sat at a table by the window. They were sharing a pizza. The woman ate daintily with a knife and fork. The men used their fingers and talked with their mouths full.

At a table near the take-out counter were two men and two women drinking coffee. The men were arguing about baseball. The women seemed bored.

At the fourth table were five young men wearing the uniform of the telephone company. They were eating submarine sandwiches and joking with a waitress.

A bearded cook appeared at the take-out counter. "What'll it be, kids?" he inquired.

"One all-the-way pizza and two large root beers, please," said Encyclopedia.

"Ready in a few minutes," said the cook. "You can wait over there."

He pointed to a bench next to the cash register. Encyclopedia and Sally sat down, their backs to the tables.

"Something funny is going on here," whispered Sally.

"I didn't notice anything," replied Encyclopedia. "What is it?"

Sally shrugged uneasily. "I'm not sure. I can't quite put my finger on it."

A few minutes later, the beefy woman in brown and the slender man stopped at the cash register. They paid their check and left.

The next to depart were the five telephone-company men. As they stopped to pay, a scream sounded from the rear of the restaurant.

"Trouble," said one of the men. He dropped two bills hastily by the cash register. "Let's get out of here."

"Police! Call the police!" a woman screamed.

The bearded cook rushed to the telephone.

While the bearded cook rushed to a telephone, the rest of the customers rushed for the
door. No one wanted to get involved.

Within three minutes Officer Carlson drove
up in a patrol car. Encyclopedia and Sally followed him to a large table in the rear.

Seated around the table were the only persons
remaining in the restaurant: the bearded cook,
two waitresses, Mario himself, and a dark-haired
young woman with a bruise on her jaw.

They all started chattering at the sight of
Officer Carlson. He had trouble quieting them.
It was a while before he was able to piece to-
gether what had happened.

Every Tuesday Mario had the cash from the
business put in the bank. The dark-haired
young woman was his daughter, Isabel. As it
was Tuesday, she had started for the bank with
the money in an envelope in her purse. She
never got there.

"I stopped in the ladies' room to freshen my
makeup," she said. "I heard the door open be-

hind me. The only thing I ever saw was a fist."

A waitress had discovered her on the floor, unconscious. Her pocketbook lay open. The envelope with the money was gone.

Officer Carlson said, "Who knew about the weekly trips to the bank?"

"Everyone here," answered Mario, a short, friendly man. "But I trust them all. . . . Wait! John Rizzo knew. He was my cook. I fired him last week."

"Did you see him today?" asked Officer Carlson.

"No," said Mario heavily.

Officer Carlson looked around. "The door to the ladies' room can be seen from any of the tables," he said. "So the thief knew when Isabel entered it."

"The thief can't be a woman," said Mario. "No woman could knock out my Isabel with one punch. Isabel can carry a fifty-pound sack of flour under each arm. She is very, very strong."

"And the thief can't be a man," said Officer Carlson. "A man certainly would have caused an outcry going into the ladies' room. He wouldn't have risked it."

"So who does that leave?" exclaimed Mario.

"John Rizzo," said Sally.

"You know him?" said Mario in surprise.

"No," said Sally. "But you said that he knew about the weekly trips to the bank."

"I don't see how you can decide that John Rizzo is the thief," said Encyclopedia.

"That's because you are a boy," answered Sally. "And boys today haven't learned their manners."

WHAT HAD SALLY SEEN?

(Turn to page 91 for the solution to The Case of the Mysterious Thief.)

The Case of the Old Calendars

Sally brought the news when she returned from lunch. "Butch Mulligan is in a fight at his house!"

Butch Mulligan was eighteen. His neck measured eighteen inches—around, not high. His arms looked as if they were made of steel cables.

"Who's dumb enough to fight Butch?" asked Encyclopedia.

"Bugs Meany and his Tigers," answered Sally gleefully.

"Hot dog!" exclaimed Encyclopedia and rushed for his bike.

A crowd of neighborhood children watched the action and urged the Tigers to keep on fighting.

Butch lived on Suncrest Drive. When the detectives rode up, he was defending the steps that led down to the basement at the side of his house.

A crowd of neighborhood children watched the action and urged the Tigers to keep on fighting. Whenever a Tiger was sent whistling through the air, the children egged him on with cries of "More! More!"

As the detectives joined the crowd, two Tigers pulled themselves off the grass. They muttered to each other and charged Butch.

A swift kick in the shin greeted the first Tiger. He yelped, hopped backward, and fell to the ground.

"You kick them, and you don't hurt your hands," Butch explained to the crowd.

"Far out!" cried Millie Davis.

The second Tiger hissed, snorted, and leaped. He struck Butch with his shoulder and they both slipped to the bottom step. Butch recovered quickly. He pinned the Tiger's arm and carried him back upstairs.

"I don't mind the stairs," Butch announced. "They keep the legs in shape."

"Butch, you're beautiful!" hollered Tim Shaw. "You can do it all!"

Everyone in the crowd cheered except Encyclopedia. He was trying to learn how the battle had started.

He finally spied Haystacks Mulligan, Butch's little brother, in the back of the crowd. "What's going on?" the detective inquired.

"Bugs tried to cheat Butch out of a calendar," said Haystacks.

He explained that Mr. Downing, the math teacher, had moved to Michigan yesterday. Before he left, he had given twenty-five old wall calendars to Butch.

"Each calendar has a big picture of a Civil War battle on it," said Haystacks. "They're really neat!"

"How does Bugs figure in?" asked Encyclopedia.

"Bugs says he had asked for the calendars last week, but Mr. Downing forgot. So, according to Bugs, Mr. Downing gave him a note yesterday morning before he left Idaville. The note instructs Butch to give half the calendars to Bugs."

Haystacks drew a slip of paper from his pocket and passed it to Encyclopedia. It read:

Dear Butch:

I forgot that I promised the calendars to Bugs Meany. Therefore, so that you may each have the same number, please divide the 25 calendars by ½.

John Downing

Haystacks said, "An hour ago Bugs showed up with the note. Butch took him to the basement and divided the twenty-five calendars. He kept twelve and gave Bugs twelve. That left one calendar."

"Cutting it in half wouldn't have been right," said Encyclopedia.

"They decided to toss a coin for it," said Haystacks. "Butch called heads. Bugs flipped a nickel and slapped it onto his wrist."

"Bugs said it landed tails," guessed Encyclopedia. "And Butch never got a chance to see for himself."

"You're right as rain," said Haystacks. "Butch became disgusted. He threw Bugs and his twelve calendars out the basement door."

Haystacks paused to watch a Tiger sail off Butch's foot.

Then he continued. "Bugs screamed that nobody gets away with cheating him. He told his Tigers to gang up on Butch and teach him a lesson."

"Somebody's getting a lesson, all right," said Encyclopedia.

A Tiger had jumped down behind Butch, where he suddenly realized he had no help. Butch went for him, grabbed his ankles and dragged him upstairs, bumpety-bump.

"When the head bangs on the steps, the brain

thinks twice," Butch commented. He laughed.

He flung the Tiger beneath a tree, and Dave Fine whooped. "That makes twenty-one!" Dave was keeping count of the knockdowns.

"Butch is drawing close," said Nick Harmon. Nick's hobby was world records. "Last year a saloonkeeper in England threw out eight drunks twenty-two times."

"Butch can't break that record," insisted Ken Wilson, who would argue with an echo. "The Englishman handled the real goods. These are kids. They're pretty skinny."

"Yes, but they're mean," said Marcia Smith. "And remember the steps. Butch is working uphill."

Bugs and Rocky Graham, the only two Tigers able to walk, wobbled toward Butch.

The crowd stilled. Everyone sensed a record in the making. It was like following a no-hitter into the ninth inning.

Butch broke the record as Sally reached Encyclopedia's side. "Whatever made Butch so angry?" she gasped.

"If you think he's angry now," said Ency-clopedia, "wait till he learns how Bugs tricked him!"

WHAT DID ENCYCLOPEDIA MEAN?

(Turn to page 92 for the solution to The Case of the Old Calendars.)

The Case of Lightfoot Louie

The state worm-racing championship was only two days off when Thad Dixon entered the Brown Detective Agency. He was walking.

Encyclopedia was very surprised to see an upright Thad. When the worm-racing season began, Thad usually went about on his hands and knees, searching for fast steppers.

"Gosh, Thad," said Encyclopedia. "I didn't expect to see you till after the big race. I thought you'd be using every minute to get Sis-Boom-Bah in shape."

Sis-Boom-Bah was Thad's wonder worm. The slim, five-inch athlete had fairly coasted to victory in the area trials a week ago.

Thad bowed his head. "Last Monday Sis-Boom-Bah went to that big mud hole in the sky," he said sadly. "I stepped on him by mistake."

"How awful," exclaimed Sally.

Thad dug into his pocket for a quarter.

"I want to hire you," he said. "I have to judge a worm today."

He explained. With Sis-Boom-Bah dead, a lot of boys and girls had seen the chance to win the state championships.

To handle the rush of late entries, the Worm Racers' Club of America had ruled that any club member could clock a worm's speed. If fast enough, the worm would be allowed to enter the statewide race.

"I'm the club's man in Idaville," said Thad proudly. "So far this week I've turned down six worms and okayed one. Today I have to time Hoager Dempsey's racer Lightfoot Louie."

"What is Hoager doing training worms?" asked Sally. "He hates animals."

"The owner of the winning worm gets a hundred-dollar savings bond this year," said Thad. "If I don't pass Lightfoot Louie, Hoager will get mad. He might even clap me on the ears with my own ankles. So I want you along."

Before Encyclopedia could talk his way out of the case, Sally had accepted it. She had never liked Hoager, who was twelve and mean for his age.

Half an hour later, Thad cleared his throat as he stood in Hoager's backyard. "We've come to time Lightfoot Louie," he said. "Shall we begin?"

"You're the boss, worm man," replied Hoager.

He dragged over an outdoor table. On it he placed a clear plastic tube a foot long and an inch wide. One end was closed by a wad of paper.

"The tube makes a perfect racecourse, don't you agree?" said Hoager, showing his teeth.

"Er . . . y-yes," stammered Thad, and hastily he explained the rules. There was only one.

To qualify for the championship race, a worm had to travel five feet at a speed no slower than six hundred hours per mile.

"Lightfoot Louie can beat that waltzing," bragged Hoager. He drew the worm from his pocket and slid him in the open end of the tube.

"Runner ready," observed Thad, clearing his stopwatch. "On your mark . . . get set . . . go!"

It wasn't go. It wasn't slow. It wasn't anything. Lightfoot Louie didn't move. He lay there like a wet shoelace.

"There's too much sunlight," said Hoager. "He's sleepy."

Hoager wrapped an old towel around the tube, hiding the racecourse completely. Next he shoved Lightfoot Louie farther into the tube. As soon as the worm disappeared, Hoager shouted, "What a start!"

"How do I know?" complained Thad. "I can't see a thing."

Hoager fixed Thad with the eye of a shark. "Don't talk about missing the action, friend," he warned. "I'll describe it to you."

"S-s-s-sure, H-Hoager," Thad agreed. "S-sure."

Hoager squinted into the tube. "Will you look at that little rascal go!"

For a few minutes Hoager kept up a running account of the worm's efforts within the covered tube. Twice he plugged the open end with his thumb. This, he explained, was to keep Lightfoot Louie from falling out while making a turn.

Eventually, Hoager grew weary of describing Lightfoot Louie's progress. He fell silent.

Minute after minute dragged by. Thad could stand it no longer.

"Where is he now?" he asked.

"Making his turn at the far end," Hoager reported. "Talk about smooth . . . unbelievable!"

Hoager squinted into the tube. "Will you look at that
little rascal go!"

"Unbelievable says it all," grumbled Sally.

"He's on the last lap now," cried Hoager. "Here he comes . . . Wow! What a finish! Fantastic!"

He pulled Lightfoot Louie from the open end. "This little speed merchant breezed into the championship race," he said. "Isn't that correct, Mr. Timekeeper?"

"*You* breezed into the championship all right," said Sally. "For liars!"

"Nobody calls me a liar," growled Hoager.

He swung at Sally's chin and went "Oooof!" Sally had landed a left to his stomach. He swung again and went *thud!* Sally had dumped him on his pants with an uppercut.

All at once she looked worried. She turned to Encyclopedia.

"You can prove that he made up the whole race, can't you?" she said.

"Of course," said the detective.

WHAT WAS THE PROOF?

(*Turn to page 93 for the solution to The Case of Lightfoot Louie.*)

The Case of the Broken Window

It was eight thirty at night when John Hall telephoned Chief Brown.

Fifteen minutes later Encyclopedia and his father were driving to Mr. Hall's house. Encyclopedia wore his Halloween pirate's costume. Chief Brown was dressed as a caveman.

"Mr. Hall is giving a costume party tonight," said Chief Brown. "That's the reason for our dressing up. He doesn't want his guests alarmed by the sight of the police."

"What happened?" asked Encyclopedia. He

had been too excited at going along on a grown-up case to ask questions before now.

"Someone, perhaps a guest, stole a valuable stamp," answered Chief Brown.

Mr. Hall had the largest stamp collection in Idaville. Some of his stamps were worth thousands of dollars.

He was waiting outside his house when Encyclopedia and Chief Brown drove up at quarter past nine.

The two men shook hands, and Chief Brown said, "This is my son Leroy. I hope you don't mind that I brought him."

"Your son?" exclaimed Mr. Hall. "Why, I thought he was a real pirate!"

Encyclopedia gritted his teeth and followed the men into the house. They walked past groups of costumed guests and up a flight of stairs.

"In here," said Mr. Hall, entering his study. The room's one window was open. The glass was shattered.

Mr. Hall stopped by the desk, on which lay a stamp album. In a calm voice he told what had happened.

At seven o'clock he had taken the stamp album from the wall safe to enjoy it. At eight o'clock the first guest had arrived, and he had gone downstairs. He had locked the door and window, but had left the album out on the desk.

Shortly after eight thirty, he had gone back upstairs to put the album in the safe. He had found the door unlocked and the window broken.

"So far as I can tell at the moment, the only thing missing is the Louis Guinea, a French stamp worth ten thousand dollars," he said.

"The thief probably first sneaked up the stairs and found the door locked," said Chief Brown. "So he went into the backyard and climbed that little tree and broke in. It was already dark, and so he was pretty sure no one would see him. He stole the stamp and left by unlocking the door from the inside."

"I quite agree," said Mr. Hall. "The tree is small and shaky. The thief must have decided there was less risk in leaving the room by the staircase."

"That makes him a guest—someone in costume," said Chief Brown. "If he had been questioned on the stairs, he could always say that he had heard a noise and came upstairs to investigate. Has anyone left the party?"

"No, I checked," said Mr. Hall. "All the guests are still here. The thief won't dare call attention to himself by leaving early."

"There is no point to searching everyone," said Chief Brown. "If the thief got wind of a search, he would get rid of the stamp in a second."

"Or worse, destroy it rather than be caught," said Mr. Hall. "That's why I asked you to wear a costume. You can do your work without drawing attention."

Mr. Hall replaced the stamp album in the wall safe.

"I haven't moved anything but the album," he said. "Now, please excuse me. I must rejoin my guests."

After he had gone, Encyclopedia walked to the desk. It was bare except for a pair of tweezers and a bottle of benzine with an eyedropper for finding watermarks. A quartz lamp stood behind the desk chair.

"Leroy, over here," called Chief Brown.

He held up a tiny bit of curved glass. It had fallen among the flat window glass on the carpet.

"It could be from an eyeglass lens," he said. "The thief might have broken his glasses getting into the room."

"Then we better look for a man wearing broken eyeglasses," said Encyclopedia. "Or, if he's taken them off, for someone who squints and bumps into things."

Father and son went downstairs. They decided to separate and meet in the kitchen in half an hour.

Encyclopedia moved slowly among the

"Leroy, over here," called Chief Brown. He held up a tiny bit of curved glass.

many colorfully costumed men and women.

A floppy horse brushed past him. "The man in the rear could have glasses on, broken or not," thought Encyclopedia. "But how to find out?"

A man dressed as the great detective Sherlock Holmes—with a deerstalker cap, magnifying glass, and pipe—was reading a poem to a ballerina.

He was reading, however, without the help of eyeglasses or the magnifying glass, and it was the ballerina who squinted.

"No, she's just fluttering her eyelashes," Encyclopedia realized when he moved closer.

A Humpty-Dumpty sat on a chair and peered through blinking red eyes.

"He's just tipsy," Encyclopedia decided as Humpty-Dumpty fell off his chair. He lay on the floor snoring.

At the end of half an hour, the boy detective had seen no one with broken eyeglasses or a squint. He headed to the kitchen. On the way he sidestepped a masked man in a cowboy outfit.

Chief Brown was waiting by the stove. "I hope you did better than I," he said. "I struck out."

"Struck . . . that's it, Dad!" exclaimed Encyclopedia. "That bit of curved glass wasn't from an eyeglass lens at all!"

WHAT DID ENCYCLOPEDIA MEAN?

(Turn to page 94 for the solution to The Case of the Broken Window.)

The Case of the Gasoline Pill

Twinkletoes Willis was Idaville's greatest child track star.

Eight years ago he had run a 50-yard dash, and the country had taken notice. His time, 22.1 seconds, had set an American record for boys under two years of age.

Ever since then, Twinkletoes seldom walked if he could run. When he came into the Brown Detective Agency, however, he wasn't running. He was limping.

"My left foot is killing me," he groaned.

"Maybe you have a hole in your shoe," said Sally.

"Naw, the hole is in my right shoe," replied Twinkletoes. "I've got my money roll in my left, and is it making my toes sore!"

"You've found a new way of footing your bills," remarked Encyclopedia. "How come?"

Twinkletoes explained. Half an hour ago he had gone to Mr. Arronzi's shoemaker's shop to have the hole fixed. But Mr. Arronzi was so busy that he couldn't start new work for two days.

"While I was there," said Twinkletoes, "Wilford Wiggins walked in."

"Oh, oh," said Encyclopedia.

Wilford Wiggins was a high school dropout and as lazy as a curbstone. His mother wasn't sure how tall he was. She hardly ever saw him standing up.

Wilford spent his time lying in bed and dreaming up get-rich-quick ideas. At least once a week, Encyclopedia had to stop him from cheating the children of the neighborhood.

"What was Wilford doing at the shoe-maker's?" asked Sally. "He's so seldom on his feet."

"He left a pair of boots. They needed heels," said Twinkletoes. "He was surprised to see me."

"Why?" asked Sally.

"Wilford thought I'd be at the city dump," replied Twinkletoes. "He's called a secret meeting there for two o'clock. I hadn't heard about it because I've been out of town."

Encyclopedia nodded knowingly. "Wilford told you to race home and get all your money and bring it to the meeting."

"Right," said Twinkletoes. "I ran home and got my life savings—twelve dollars. Wilford has a new plan to make us little kids richer than millionaires."

He laid a quarter on the gas can beside Encyclopedia.

"I stuck my money roll in my shoe to keep it safe, but it's slowed me down," he said. "I need a bodyguard."

Encyclopedia returned the quarter. "No

charge," he said, "in a case involving Wilford."

"I know Wilford is so crooked he can hide in the shadow of a wishbone," said Twinkletoes. "But this time he may be on the up-and-up."

"We'll have to hurry to find out," said Sally. "It's nearly two o'clock."

When the detectives and Twinkletoes reached the city dump, the secret meeting was about to start. A crowd of children pressed around Wilford.

"Move in closer," he called. "I don't want anyone but my friends to hear this. I'm going to make you so rich that when you catch cold, you can go to two nose doctors—one for each nostril!"

"Aw, can the balloon juice," hollered Bugs Meany, "before your tongue gets sunburned. Let's have it straight. What's the big deal?"

"Can't wait, eh, kid?" said Wilford. He fished in his pocket. "Okay, here it is!"

He held up a red pill.

"What is it, you ask?" he cried. "It's a gas

The secret meeting was about to start. A crowd of children pressed around Wilford.

saver! One pill in a tank of gas will give up to a thousand miles of driving!"

"That's the greatest invention since sliced bread," Twinkletoes whispered to Encyclopedia.

"This little wonder is the brain child of Dr. Pablo Mann of Brazil," Wilford announced. "It's not quite ready to market. Dr. Mann needs two more years to perfect it."

"So what are you selling?" someone shouted.

"Opportunity," answered Wilford. "The opportunity for each of you to get in on the ground floor—cheap. One share of the business for ten dollars. Buy as many shares as you wish."

"If the pill really will work, why don't you buy all the shares yourself?" asked Twinkletoes.

"Because I'm flying down to Brazil right after this meeting," replied Wilford. "On the way to the airport, I'll have to stop at the bank and draw out all my savings just to pay for the plane ticket."

"Let's see your wallet," said Encyclopedia. "I bet you have lots of money."

Wilford tossed Encyclopedia his wallet. "Satisfy yourself, Mr. Smarty Detective, even though you weren't invited here."

Inside the wallet Encyclopedia found a driver's license, a claim ticket from the shoemaker, an old theater stub, and three postage stamps. But only seven dollars.

While Encyclopedia was examining the wallet, Wilford continued his sales pitch.

"I'll be gone a year, maybe two, helping Dr. Mann in his hidden laboratory in the jungle," he said. "Before I leave, I want all my young friends to have this chance of a lifetime—"

"To lose every cent they give you," snapped Encyclopedia.

WHAT MADE ENCYCLOPEDIA
SO SURE?

(*Turn to page 95 for the solution to The Case of the Gasoline Pill.*)

The Case of the Pantry Door

Hilda Deaderick, also known as Deadeye Deaderick, was Idaville's only girl fly hunter.

"Fly hunting may seem a little weird to non-hunters," she said, sitting in the Brown Detective Agency. "But it's a hobby that grows on you."

Hilda sneered at sprays and flyswatters. Sprays were smelly. Flyswatters were messy. Neither was sporting.

She used rubber bands only. Like any good hunter, she moved carefully till—*zap!* From two feet away she was deadly.

"I stopped by to invite you to a birthday party for Archie," she said to the detectives. "I'm serving him flies and bits of bacon in an hour."

"How marvelous!" exclaimed Sally. "We'd love to come."

"You're the guests of honor," said Hilda.

The titles had been earned. A year ago, Encyclopedia had discovered the frog in the birdhouse in Hilda's backyard. Sally had named him Archie.

No one had yet figured out why a frog had chosen to live in a birdhouse atop a pole.

"Maybe he decided to wait for the rent on lily pads to go down," suggested Encyclopedia as he closed the detective agency.

"Archie probably got into the birdhouse as a tadpole," said Sally. "Now he's grown too big to get out."

"No one knows just how big he is," said Hilda. "He never sticks out more than his head and front feet. But I guess he's the size of a jelly doughnut."

Hilda laid the fly on the tiny porch of the birdhouse.

They reached Hilda's street. Encyclopedia noticed two Tigers, Rocky Graham and Duke Kelly, throwing a football down the block.

Hilda paused on the way to her backyard to shoot a fly in midair. She laid it on the tiny porch of the birdhouse.

Out of the round opening snaked a long tongue. The fly disappeared.

"Archie has given meaning to my hobby," said Hilda. "Before he came to live here, I was getting bored."

"What do you mean?" asked Sally.

"I never missed," said Hilda. "Oh, in the beginning I had to use thick rubber bands—at least an eighth of an inch wide. The skinny ones were less accurate. But soon I went to the skinnies to give a fly an even chance."

"That's style," murmured Sally.

"Next I broke rubber bands and snapped flies with one end," said Hilda. "I had to be six inches or less from the victim. I still got my flies. It was boring."

"Until Archie turned everything around," said Sally.

"Yes," said Hilda. "He made me feel needed."

She led the detectives into the house. A girl of about fourteen sat at the kitchen table eating grapes.

"This is my cousin Lois," said Hilda. "She's staying with us for a week."

Lois continued to stuff in grapes with both hands. She mumbled, "Hello," without missing a stuff.

"We're getting up a birthday feast for Archie," Hilda told her. "Bacon bits and flies."

"Yuuuuck!" said Lois.

Hilda ignored the remark. She got four saucers from a cabinet above the sink and asked the detectives to fill them with sugar.

"I'm going hunting in the attic," she said. "By the time I've worked my way downstairs, the flies should have found the sugar. Then, bang, bang, bang!"

She pointed to a door. "The sugar is in the pantry," she added. "The door may give you a hard time."

After she left, Encyclopedia tried to open the door. It was stuck. He pushed on it and pounded.

"What a racket! You're giving me a headache!" whined Lois. She swept from the kitchen with the bowl of grapes.

Another minute of pounding and the door came unstuck. The pantry was a deep, narrow room lined with shelves of food. The detectives stepped into it, looking for the sugar.

Suddenly the door closed behind them. The bolt screeched shut, locking them in darkness.

"What the—?" gasped Sally.

Footsteps sounded, running toward the front of the house. A door slammed.

"That sounded like the front door." said Encyclopedia. He began to pound on the locked pantry door.

"All right, I hear you!" screamed Lois

from the floor above. "Hold your horses. I'm coming!"

She had the detectives freed by the time Hilda dashed into the kitchen. "What's going on?" Hilda asked.

"Someone locked us in the pantry," said Encyclopedia.

Hilda looked astonished—until she noticed the cabinet door above the sink was open.

"The money is gone!" she cried. "My mother keeps household cash in this glass jar. It was filled when I got out the four saucers. Now it's empty!"

"Just after I went up to my room, I heard the front door slam," said Lois. "I looked out the window and saw a boy running toward the street."

"Rocky Graham and Duke Kelly were throwing a football when we got here," said Sally. "Either could be the thief."

"It might have been anybody—anybody

who knew where the money was kept," said Hilda.

"No, not anybody," said Encyclopedia. "The thief is—"

WHO?

(Turn to page 96 for the solution to The Case of the Pantry Door.)

Solution to *The Case of the Dead Eagles*

Mike said that the year before he had not been looking at the eagles or their nest. He had simply been admiring the full moon, which was "right above the cliff."

Standing on the same path, Encyclopedia and Charlie had seen the setting sun atop the cliff.

So they all had been facing west.

Unfortunately for Mike's alibi, the full moon is never seen in the western sky at night!

Trapped by his own words, Mike admitted killing the three eagles. He promised to spare the mother eagle and her eggs if the boys did not tell on him.

The boys kept their word. Mike kept his.

Solution to *The Case of the Hypnotism Lesson*

Bugs didn't know any more about hynotizing a lobster than he knew about steering a spacecraft to Mars.

The color photograph was the proof.

It showed Bugs holding up "a large red lobster by the tail."

Living lobsters, however, are not red.

They turn red only after they have been cooked!

So the lobster that Dave paid to see hypnotized was already boiled and dead when Bugs took his money.

"No wonder I couldn't make it stand on its head!" exclaimed Bugs. "I'll give you the hypnotizing course for fifty cents a lesson to make up for my mistake."

"No, thanks," said Dave. He got back his dollar.

Solution to *The Case of the Parking Meters*

According to Bugs's story, Sally had stolen the reel of film as soon as it ended. That is, before Bugs had a chance to rewind it.

And he did not rewind it in front of Officer Culp and the detectives in his house.

Had Sally really stolen the film as Bugs claimed, it would have appeared upside down and backward when Bugs showed it to Officer Culp and the detectives.

Encyclopedia pointed this out, and Bugs confessed. He had written the Robin Hood card himself.

One of his Tigers had made the telephone calls to Encyclopedia and Sally. Another Tiger had posed as the boy detective in the movie.

Solution to *The Case of the Hidden Will*

The first clue was Mr. King's basement, on whose walls hung enlarged framed pictures of every playing card in the deck.

The second clue was the poem. The first "King" was written with a capital K since it stood for the family name. The second "king" was written with a small k, and so it stood for something else—like a card.

The third clue was the description of Mr. King's four sons. Only Frank did not have a moustache.

The will, Encyclopedia realized, was framed in with the picture of the king of hearts, the only king that doesn't have a moustache.

There it was found. And Frank, the thieving son, inherited nothing.

Solution to *The Case of the Mysterious Thief*

The thief had to look like a woman and punch like a man. In short, a man dressed as a woman!

John Rizzo had dressed as a woman, and his wife had dressed as a man. Sally's clue was their positions at the table.

When a man and a woman sit at a table for two by the wall, good manners call for the woman to face out so she can see and be seen. The man faces the wall.

But Mrs. Rizzo, dressed as the man, had sat with her back to the wall. She needed a full view of the restaurant in order to act as a lookout while her husband stole the money.

Only Sally remembered that the beefy "woman" and the slender "man" had sat in the wrong places.

Thanks to Sally, the Rizzos were caught.

Solution to *The Case of the Old Calendars*

Encyclopedia meant that sooner or later Butch would realize that Bugs had forged the note asking him to divide the twenty-five calendars evenly.

Alas for Bugs, he made an error in math. Encyclopedia spotted the error right away, and so he knew the note was a fake.

Mr. Downing, a math teacher, never would have written ". . . divide the 25 calendars by ½."

Why not? Because 25 divided by ½ is 50, not 12½! (25 divided by 2 is 12½.)

When Butch finally realized that the note was forged, he took back the twelve calendars from Bugs—and set another record for knockdowns.

Solution to *The Case of Lightfoot Louie*

Lightfoot Louie had to travel a distance of five feet. The tube was one foot long. So he had to travel five laps.

At the finish, Hoager had cried, "He's on the last lap now. . . . Here he comes. . . ." Then he pulled the worm from the open end, or starting point.

However, the worm could have finished at the same end at which it started only by racing even laps—2, 4, 6, and so on.

Starting at the open end, Lightfoot Louie would have finished the five laps at the opposite, or closed, end.

Caught in his mistake, Hoager confessed. He had made up the entire race. Lightfoot Louie hadn't budged an inch.

Solution to *The Case of the Broken Window*

Mr. Hall was too upset by the theft of the stamp to notice that something else was missing from his desk.

It was something used in looking at stamps—a magnifying glass.

The thief had broken his magnifying glass when he struck the window with it. He had picked up all the pieces except one from the carpet and dropped them, with the frame, onto the ground below.

To maintain his costume, he had stolen Mr. Hall's magnifying glass along with the stamp.

Mr. Hall found the magnifying glass where Encyclopedia reasoned it was—in the hand of "Sherlock Holmes."

The stolen stamp was found in "Holmes's" wallet.

Solution to *The Case of the Gasoline Pill*

Encyclopedia had asked to see Wilford's wallet, but not to find out how much money he had.

The detective wanted to see if a shoemaker's claim ticket was in it. It was.

Mr. Arronzi, the shoemaker, had told Twinkle-toes that he was too busy to mend any more shoes for two days.

Yet Wilford had left his boots to have new heels put on.

So Wilford lied about getting on a plane that very day and flying to Brazil for a year or two.

The claim ticket told Encyclopedia the truth. Wilford fully expected to be in Idaville to pick up his boots in two days.

Solution to *The Case of the Pantry Door*

The thief was Lois.

After leaving the kitchen, she had slipped back, locked the detectives in the pantry, and stolen the money.

Then she had run to the front door and slammed it. She wanted Encyclopedia to believe that the thief had fled the house.

Finally, she had sneaked upstairs. To prove where she was, she had answered Encyclopedia's pounding by shouting, "All right, I hear you! Hold your horses. I'm coming!"

That was her mistake! Only if she knew that Encyclopedia needed help would she have called, "I'm coming!"

Had she been innocent, she would have thought he was trying to get *into* the pantry, not *out!*